All About Salt

Heather Hammonds

Contents

Salt

Salt is used every day by people all around the world.

Salt is a **mineral**. Some kinds of salt are eaten by people and animals.

Salt is also used in other ways.

Salt is found in many different places on Earth.
In some places it is found on land.
In other places it is found in water.

Salt is also called sodium chloride (say: *so-dee-um klor-ide*).

This salt has been collected from the sea.

How Salt Is Used

Salt is often used in cooking, or sprinkled on food. Adding salt to some foods can make them taste better.

The salt may be made up of small **crystals** or larger crystals. It may even be different colours.

Salt can be sprinkled on some foods.

These are all different kinds of salt.

In some places, salt is sprinkled on roads in very cold weather.
It helps to stop dangerous ice forming on the roads.

A truck sprinkles salt on the road.

Collecting and Mining Salt

Salt is collected from water and land in different ways.

Sea Salt

Sea salt is collected from seawater.
Sea salt farms are built near the seashore.

Salty water is pumped from the sea into huge ponds.
The sun and wind slowly dry up the water in the ponds.
The salt is left behind.

Sea salt is also called **solar** salt, because it is collected using the sun.

Salt has been piled up in ponds at this sea salt farm.

Huge machines are used to collect the salt from the salt ponds.
The salt is washed until it is clean.
Then it is dried.

Salt is collected from a salt pond with a huge machine.

Rock Salt

Rock salt is dug out from deep under the ground, at salt mines.

Miners dig long tunnels through the salt, inside the mines.
The tunnels are big enough for miners to drive trucks and other machines through.

Miners use the machines to dig out the rock salt.
Rock salt mining can be a dangerous job.
Miners drill through the salt and **blast** it out, too!

This machine is drilling through the salt in a salt mine.

People can visit some salt mines and learn about rock salt mining.

Salt Mining with Water

Salt is also mined by pumping fresh water
into rock salt, deep underground.
This kind of mining is called "solution mining".

The water goes down a long pipe
and mixes with the rock salt.
The water becomes very salty.

The salty water is pumped back up
through another pipe and into a factory.

Machines are used to dry up the water,
so the salt can be collected.

Water that is very salty
is called "brine".

A Solution Mine

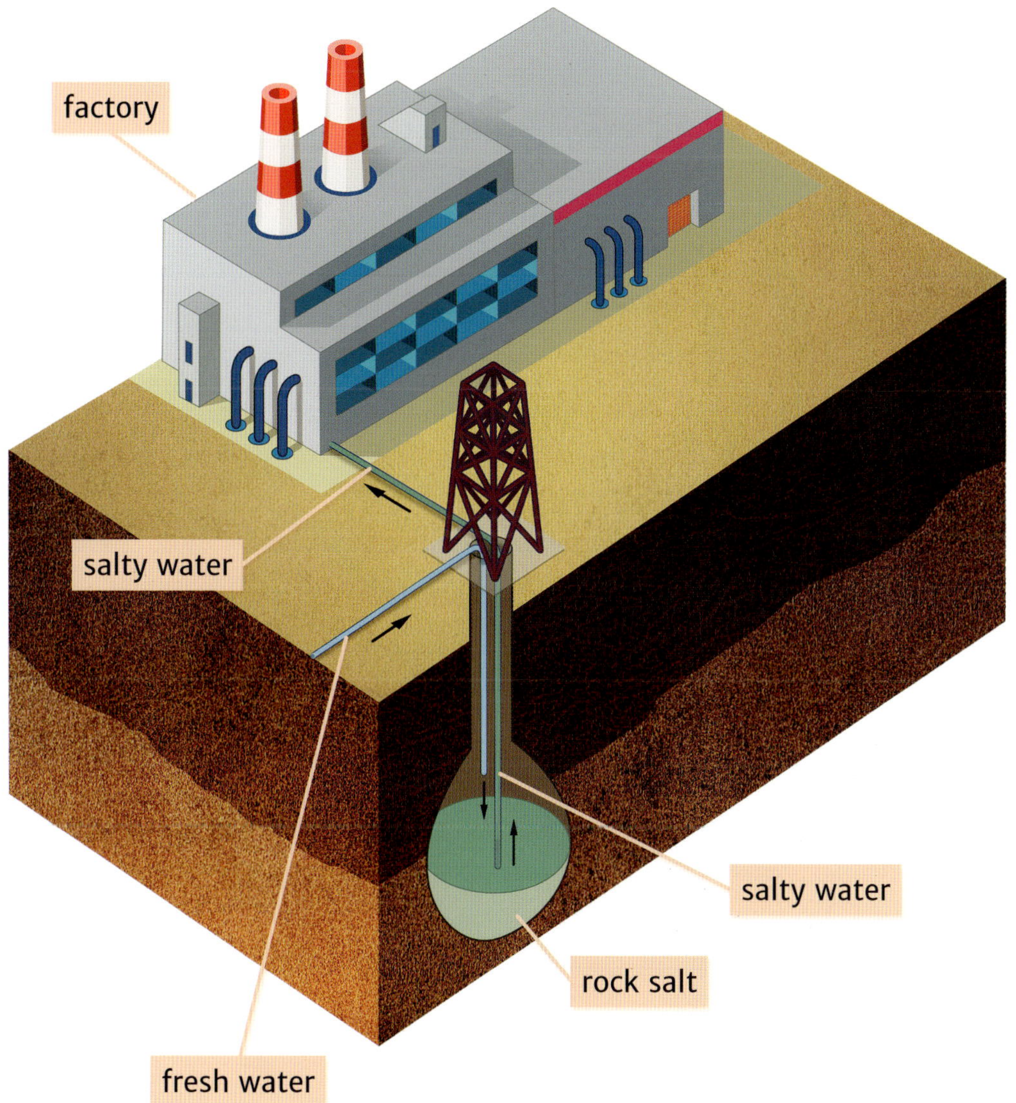

Salt and Our Health

Salt is an important part of our diet.
Our bodies cannot make salt, so we must eat a small amount to stay healthy.
Salt helps us to keep the right amount of water in our bodies. It also helps our muscles to work.

However, many people eat more salt than they need.
Too much salt is not good for us.
Over time, too much salt can make us sick.

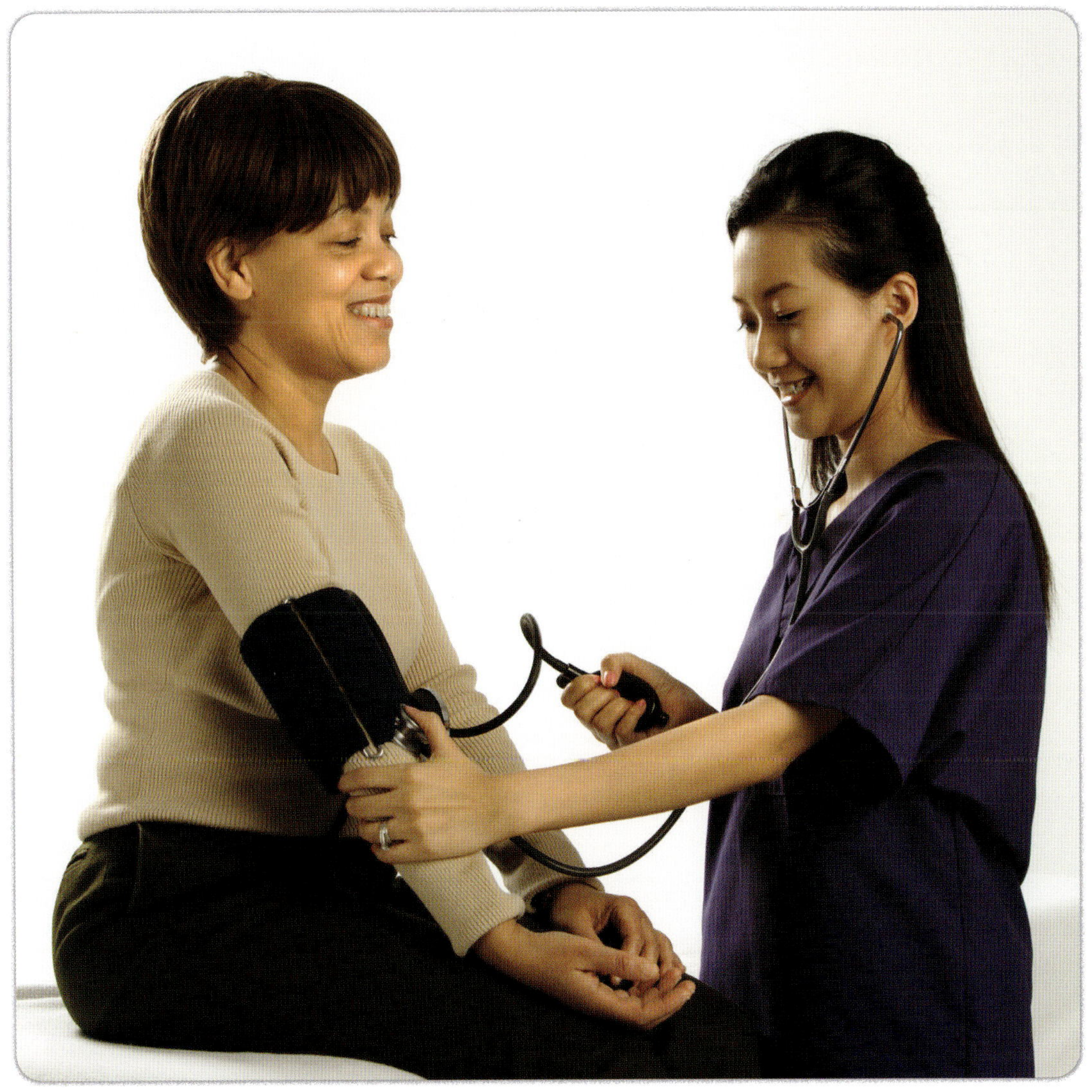

Doctors can do tests to check if people have too much salt in their bodies.

Adding salt to food can help make it taste good. Salt is found in many foods we buy.

We can easily taste the salt in some foods. However, some foods have hidden salt that is not as easy to taste.

These foods are very salty.

Fresh fruit and vegetables have less salt in them than snacks like chips.

Many foods we buy have labels on them. We can read the list of ingredients on the labels, to see how much salt is in the food.

This helps us choose foods with more or less salt in them.

Salt in the Past

Long ago, collecting and **transporting** salt was much harder than it is today. There were no big machines to collect and carry the salt.

People built roads so that salt could be transported from salt mines. It was often sent on ships to different places around the world.

Salt was **valuable** because it was hard to collect from the land and water.

Sometimes, salt was swapped for food or other goods because it was so valuable.

In some places, camels have been used for hundreds of years to transport bags of salt.

Long ago, salt was used to keep foods fresh.
There were no refrigerators or freezers
to keep foods cold.

Foods like meat were covered in salt,
or very salty water.
The salt helped stop the foods from going bad
and kept them safe to eat.

This old photo shows salted fish being packed into a barrel to keep it fresh.

Today, salt is still used to keep some foods fresh, or **preserve** them.
The salt helps make the foods taste good, too.

Salt is being used to preserve these lemons.

Cabbage is preserved with salt to make a food called "kimchi".

In the past, explorers took salted meat on ships because fresh meat would have gone bad on long journeys.

Salt and Animals

Sometimes, farm animals cannot get enough salt and other minerals from the foods they eat.

Farmers buy special blocks for their animals to lick. The blocks are made up of salt and other things the animals need to live and grow.

A cow licks a block of salt.

Lots of wild animals find places to get salt and other minerals from the ground. The animals lick and eat the dirt at these places.

A giraffe licks the salt and other minerals in a patch of dirt.

Salt is a very important mineral.
Everyone uses it in some way, almost every day.
Today, we can easily buy salt for ourselves.
But we must be careful to eat just the right amount to stay healthy.

Glossary

blast (*verb*)	to blow something up, such as rock salt, so it is in smaller pieces that can be collected
crystals (*noun*)	solid materials found on Earth that have different shapes
mineral (*noun*)	a non-living material found in or on the ground
preserve (*verb*)	to keep foods fresh for a long time
solar (*adjective*)	to do with the sun
transporting (*verb*)	taking something from place to place
valuable (*adjective*)	worth a lot of money

Index